No one ever takes Lionel Blake's ambitions seriously – which is not surprising as he has so many. In this adventure Lionel is determined to be a Private Investigator when he grows up. While travelling by train to visit Uncle Richard, Lionel overhears a conversation between two men who seem to be plotting a robbery – or worse! Piecing the clues together, he is convinced that their target is his uncle. Intent on protecting Uncle Richard, Lionel is soon involved in a web of mystery and intrigue which he not only unravels, but resolves in a most ingenious way.

Linda Allen was born in Yorkshire and now lives in Cornwall. She has been writing stories for children for many years.

Lionel
the Lone Wolf

Linda Allen

Illustrated by David Arthur

PUFFIN BOOKS

PUFFIN BOOKS

Published by the Penguin Group
27 Wrights Lane, London W8 5TZ, England
Viking Penguin Inc., 40 West 23rd Street, New York, New York 10010, USA
Penguin Books Australia Ltd, Ringwood, Victoria, Australia
Penguin Books Canada Ltd, 2801 John Street, Markham, Ontario, Canada L3R 1B4
Penguin Books (NZ) Ltd, 182–190 Wairau Road, Auckland 10, New Zealand

Penguin Books Ltd, Registered Offices: Harmondsworth, Middlesex, England

First published by Hamish Hamilton Children's Books 1988
Published in Puffin Books 1990
1 3 5 7 9 10 8 6 4 2

Made and printed in Great Britain by
Cox & Wyman Ltd, Reading, Berks.

Chapter One

"WHY doesn't anything ever happen around here?" demanded Lionel one morning at breakfast. Everybody except Lionel had a letter to read.

"Happen?" said Mum, vaguely.

"Yes, happen," repeated Lionel. "Life's so boring."

Dad glanced up from his letter. "Life ought not to be boring at your age," he said. "I'm forty-two and I haven't found life tedious yet. Why don't you take something up?"

"Like what?" asked Lionel, biting savagely on a sausage.

"Some kind of sport. I'd bet you'd be quite good at sport if you really tried. Badminton, perhaps. You have enormous stamina."

"I'm not interested in badminton."

Across the table his sister Linnet frowned at him. "You're weird," she said. "Everybody's brother but mine wants to be a big soccer star or an ace golfer. And what do you want to be? A private investigator."

"What's wrong with that?" said Lionel. "There are people who are private investigators, aren't there? What's so peculiar about it? Somebody's got to do the job. Anyhow, I can't help the way I am – I just like mysteries, that's all."

Mum leaned over and patted his hand. "Of course you can't help it, dear," she said. "I like mysteries too, and so does your father. That's why we're anthropologists. We're uncovering mysteries all the time."

"I know, Mum, but I mean real-life mysteries, not about people who lived thousands of years ago."

"Oh, but it isn't just ancient peoples we study, Lionel. Why do you think we're off to the Amazon basin at the end of next week? We're going to study the Kayapo Indians. You remember I was telling you about their legends? How they believe that their ancestors acquired the secrets of fire and weapons from the jaguar, and that . . ."

"Yes, I know, Mum, you told me, but that doesn't help me, does it?"

"I don't suppose it does," said Mum, as if she was quite taken with the idea. "I think your father's quite right, though. You should take an interest in something active."

Lionel sighed. "Being a P.I.'s active. It isn't just sitting in an office all day, you know. Anyhow, I'm no good at sport. I can't stick to the rules. So what am I supposed to do with myself when you're away?"

Mum regarded him thoughtfully over her letter. "Is that what's bothering you? You don't want us to go away? You've never felt that way before. We didn't think you minded staying at home with Grandpa and Linnet."

"I don't mind when I've got something interesting to work on," Lionel assured her, "but Linnet won't let me take people's fingerprints and she goes crazy when I listen in to conversations. How can I build up a file of information on people if I don't keep my ears open?"

Mum put down her letter and said, "You know, Lionel, your sister might have a point there. You don't actually write down things that you overhear, do you?"

"Yes, he does," interrupted Linnet. "He's got that old filing cabinet of Dad's in the garden shed, and he calls it his office. He's put a sign on the door – Lionel Blake, Private Investigator. *And* he's keeping files on all the neighbours. I think it's time somebody put a stop to it." She gave everybody a withering look and returned to her letter.

"That just shows how long it is since I went down to the bottom of the garden," Mum said. "I had no idea that you had set up shop there." She munched toast for a moment or two and then went on. "I can't think what you find to write about our neighbours, Lionel. They don't seem to do many interesting things."

"I know," sighed Lionel. "That's what I mean when I say why doesn't anything ever happen around here." Mum nodded sympathetically and picked up her letter again. Silence fell. Lionel stared at Linnet. "Being a P.I.'s better than collecting beetles," he said.

Linnet looked up. "Beetles?" she repeated.

"Yes. Like Bugsy Potter."

"Who on earth is Bugsy Potter?"

"His dad's a minister."

Mum said, "Oh, you mean *Gerald!*"

"Nobody calls him Gerald. We call him Bugsy because he collects them."

Grandpa put in a word. "I used to keep a pet earwig," he said, "in a matchbox. Had him for months." Then he went back to reading his letter.

"Bugsy collects them properly – he keeps them in glass cases in his bedroom. He goes out hunting them at the weekends. You ought to be glad I don't do *that*," finished Lionel triumphantly.

Linnet merely said, "Ugh! Doesn't anybody want to know who my letter's from?" she added.

"Of course we do, darling," said Mum. "Tell us."

"It's from Amanda."

Lionel groaned. "She's not coming here, is she?" That would be the last straw.

"If you must know," responded Linnet icily, "she wants me to go and stay with her. There's a new Egyptian exhibition on at the museum where her father works. She knows how interested I am in that subject, so she's got tickets for the exhibition. Can I go, Mum?"

"Of course you can. I had heard about the exhibition and I only wish I could spare the time to come with you, but ..."

Dad suddenly thumped the table. "Mike Bennett wants that film completed by next March!" he shouted. "Impossible, it can't be done!"

"Next March!" echoed Mum, and the two of them went off into a long discussion about deadlines and contracts and lots of things that Lionel didn't understand. He stuck his finger through the middle of a piece of toast and whirled it around. Nobody noticed.

"You'll never guess who this is from," said Grandpa, holding out his letter and chuckling. But as nobody offered to guess who it was from he went on, "It's from Jim." He nudged Dad, who was sitting next to him, and repeated, "Jim."

"Jim?" said Dad.

"Yes, you know, my cousin Jim."

"Oh, that Jim. How is he?"

"He's gone and done it at last, hang me if he hasn't."

"Done what?" asked Lionel, hoping it was something sensational like joining the Foreign Legion.

"Set up his own motorbike repair shop. He always said he would when he retired, and now he has. I'd like to see that. Oh, I'd like to see it!" He looked around at everybody. "There's no reason why I shouldn't, is there? Nothing to stop me?"

"When would you think of going?" asked Mum.

"Soon. How about tomorrow? Stay for a day or two."

"You'll have to be back before next weekend," said Linnet. "Mum and Dad are going away, remember."

"I'll be back before then." He was obviously very excited. Tapping the letter with his bony finger he said, "Jim says to go any time, so I'll just give him a call tonight and say I'm coming. How about coming with me, Lionel?"

"What a good idea!" said Mum. "It would make a nice change for you."

Lionel shook his head. Uncle Jim was all right, but there was also Aunt Essie, who had a mania for cleaning. She was always telling people to wipe their feet, always polishing, always scrubbing the doorstep. Besides that, she seemed to think that the whole of the human race had been put on earth for the purpose of annoying her. She didn't care for her relations very much, and she hated strangers. Lionel had never been so miserable in his life as when he had gone to visit her, but Grandpa seemed to have forgotten all that in his enthusiasm for Uncle Jim's new venture. "Well?" he said to Lionel.

"I don't want to go."

Grandpa looked hurt.

Mum folded up her letter and replaced it in the envelope. Lionel recognised the handwriting. It was Uncle Richard's. She said, "Do go with Grandpa, Lionel. If he goes to visit Uncle Jim, and Linnet goes to stay with Amanda you'll be more on your own than ever, because Dad and I will have to put in every minute we can before we go away on that film project. I'm sorry, Lionel, but we do have a contract and we can't break it now, but in future we'll consider your point of view a bit more. I promise." She still thought he was worrying about them going away.

Lionel gave Grandpa a little smile of apology, then turned to Mum and said, "Is your letter from Uncle Richard?"

"Yes, it is, and I must say it's given me a twinge of conscience. I seem to be neglecting everybody these days. I absolutely promised to go and take a look at Richard's new orchid house, and now it will be October at the very earliest before I can see it. Poor Richard. He must have felt very lonely since Maria died."

Lionel could hardly remember Aunt Maria, but he knew that Uncle Richard had moved away from the place where they had lived and started a new life in Dearmouth, a pretty seaside town. Lionel had been there once. Uncle Richard was his favourite uncle. "I could go and stay with Uncle Richard for a few days," he suggested.

Mum's face brightened. "What a wonderful idea!" she exclaimed. "He'd be so pleased to have you." She looked apologetically at Grandpa. "Richard sees so little of Lionel, you know, Grandpa. Don't you think it would be a welcome change for him to have Lionel about the place for a while?"

Grandpa said of course it would and he was sorry he'd been so selfish. Lionel should go and see his uncle once in a while.

"I think that's an excellent plan," put in Dad.

"As you say, Richard is too much on his own with just his housekeeper for company. I never did understand his passion for solitude, but I'm sure Lionel does. They're two of a kind, just happy to be pursuing their own ideas. Lone wolves."

A lone wolf! What a wonderful description! Everybody in the family had always said that Lionel resembled Uncle Richard more than anyone else, and Lionel himself was aware that it was true. Uncle Richard understood him. He'd leave him alone when he wanted to be left alone. He wouldn't interfere in what he did or laugh at what the others called his peculiar notions. "When can I go?" he asked.

"I'll go and phone him now," said Mum, standing up.

"That's right," said Grandpa, "give him something to think about – help him to forget his problems, poor chap." He chuckled when he said that, so Lionel asked him what problems he meant, because he didn't think they could be so bad if Grandpa found them funny. Grandpa laughed more than ever and said that Uncle

Richard would no doubt get round to telling him about them one day – maybe during his visit if Lionel behaved himself.

"Who's going to take him?" asked Linnet suddenly.

Mum paused at the door. "What?" she said.

"Lionel. Who's going to take him to Dearmouth?"

Mum and Dad looked blankly at one another.

"I will," said Grandpa, "on my new Hesketh. Then I'll go straight on to Newcastle."

"Oh no you won't," said Dad. He regarded Lionel thoughtfully for a few moments, then he seemed to make up his mind. "He can go on his own," he said, and Lionel's heart leapt for joy. "There's a through train. He's quite old enough to start being self-reliant."

Lionel gave Linnet a look of supreme superiority. She said, "You'd put the whole of the railway system at Lionel's mercy? It'll grind to a halt." But Lionel knew she was saying that because she was anxious about him. She was the one who worried about him more than anybody.

"Go and fetch the railway timetable, Lionel.

I believe the through train leaves for Dearmouth about eight-thirty in the mornings," said Dad.

Half an hour later it was all arranged. He was to travel the next morning, Grandpa was to go to Newcastle, and Linnet was going to London in two days' time. Lionel felt a good three inches taller than he had done when he went down to breakfast. He practised looking mysterious in the mirror in his bedroom. Somebody on the train would be sure to wonder who he was, and why he was travelling on his own.

Wandering down to the corner shop later that morning, Lionel reflected that things were looking up. He was free to do as he pleased. He was a lone wolf.

He slipped into the shop. He had come to buy a present for Uncle Richard, but the assistants weren't to know that. For anything they knew he might be keeping somebody under surveillance – that dark, husky type, for instance, who was buying gardening gloves. He stiffened. Why would a man like that be buying gardening gloves? He wasn't the type to do his gardening in gloves. He had a broken nose.

Lionel watched him furtively for a few minutes, then he caught sight of one of the assistants watching *him*. She'd remember him in time to come, when he was famous. "Oh yes," she'd say, "I remember Lionel Blake the famous investigator. He used to come into the shop quite regularly, and if you ask me he was in training then because he used to look so sinister."

He practised being sinister until it hurt his eyes, then he picked up a fountain pen. "I'll take this," he said to the assistant who had been watching him, "and have you any invisible ink?"

"If we have," she said, giggling, "it's quite escaped my notice."

"Never mind," he said loftily, "I'll get some from headquarters."

That would give her something to think about.

He returned home in time to hear an argument about whether Grandpa should travel by train or bus. Grandpa was all for going on his new bike but Mum wouldn't hear of that. She looked so worried that Lionel helped her out. "If you went by train, Grandpa," he said, "you'd be able to carry all those bike magazines that Uncle Jim asked you for."

Grandpa considered. "Yes," he said, "I believe you're right, Lionel." And he said he would go by train.

Afterwards Mum said she was amazed at Lionel's quick-wittedness in thinking about the magazines. That made Lionel's spirits soar even higher. It was the first time that anybody had told him he was quick-witted. He went about the house for the rest of the day trying to be equally sharp about other things, but nobody seemed to notice. Grandpa and Linnet were too busy getting things ready for their holidays and Mum and Dad were working in their study. It occurred to Lionel that he'd better do his packing, too. He got out his suitcase. One day he'd have one with a secret bottom in it, but for the moment this one would have to do. He put in the gift for Uncle Richard, a notebook and several pencils, a black hood and rubber shoes in case he had to do any tailing at night, and an old woolly hat and Mum's old sunglasses for when he needed a quick disguise.

He was ready for anything.

Chapter Two

THE train was busy, but Dad found a seat for Lionel and then jumped back on to the platform to wait for the train to pull out. There was a slight delay in leaving, so Lionel left his seat and stood at the door of the carriage talking to him. He wouldn't admit, even to himself, that he was feeling nervous. The bumping in his chest was merely the result of running for the train; they had had plenty of time but Lionel had insisted on running.

A stout man came hurrying along the platform. He was breathing hard and was rather red in the face. As he approached the door, which Dad was holding open for him, he glanced back the way he had come, almost as if he feared he was being followed. Lionel decided that that was worth noting in his pocket notebook. As he entered the compartment, Lionel observed the man's dress. There was very little out of the ordinary about it, except for his tie, which was a very bright purple colour with a curious motif composed of several letters which Lionel couldn't quite make out. He patted his pocket to make sure that he had brought his notebook. Yes, it was there all right, and when he was settled in his seat he would make a note about that tie.

The train started to move. "Goodbye, Dad, see you next week!"

Lionel went back to his seat. The coach in which he was travelling was one of the kind that had a centre aisle, with seats and a table for four persons on each side. Lionel's seat was on the aisle. Next to him, by the window, was a lady who was reading a book. Opposite her was a young man who was fast asleep, and opposite Lionel was a newspaper. There was a man behind it but Lionel hadn't seen his face yet. As he sat down he noticed that the stout man had found a seat a few tables away and was mopping his brow with a large handkerchief. Was he merely hot and out of breath, or was he sweating with fear? Lionel studied him carefully, but when the man caught him at it, Lionel averted his eyes.

He wouldn't think about home. He wouldn't wonder how far Grandpa had got on his journey to Newcastle, nor would he wish that Linnet was with him (she had wept a little when he had left, and given him some money to spend on the journey). He would think instead of the mysteries he was going to find, the glory he was going to receive when he had solved them. He would think of Uncle Richard and the hint of a secret in his life. Never again, after this, would he be the Lionel who had never been anywhere on his own. He would be a young man who had travelled and seen a bit of the world. Very gradually the dull ache in the pit of his stomach eased away. There was nothing to it, this travelling alone. One day he'd be doing it all the time.

He was just thinking of going to get a drink in the buffet car when the man opposite lowered his newspaper. He looked at his travelling companions, but as the lady made it quite plain that she didn't talk to strangers on trains, it was Lionel he addressed.

"Travelling on your own?" he asked.

"Yes," said Lionel. He was staring at the man's tie.

"Going on holiday?"

"Not exactly." It was the same tie as the stout man's!

"Visiting friends, perhaps?"

"Maybe." The same colour, the same pattern, everything!

Lionel took out his notebook and made notes in his secret code, which consisted of writing all words backwards in capital letters. 2 NEM, EMAS EIT. He wanted to write 'not travelling together' but it was difficult to write long words without writing them down the proper way first, and he didn't dare do that with the man looking on.

"Now I know what you are!" the man exclaimed, leaning forward.

"Do you?" said Lionel, trying to remain calm.

"Yes, you're a train-spotter. I used to be one myself when I was your age. I loved trains. Still do. Always travel by train whenever I can. I used to spend hours travelling about the railways. I saw all the great steam-engines, you know. *Corinthian*, *Leviathan*, *The Flying Scotsman* ..."

"You're wrong," said Lionel. "I'm not a train-spotter."

The man smiled. "Mysterious sort of chap, aren't you?" he said.

Lionel maintained a dignified silence as he studied the man's appearance. He was about Dad's age, but not so good-looking. He had small, rather greenish eyes, and a big nose. Although his hair was a sort of sandy-grey, his moustache was a darker colour. Obviously a false one. How did you spell 'moustache' backwards?

The man tried again. "Would you have any objection to telling me your name?"

"Why?" demanded Lionel suspiciously.

"I'd just like to know. I have an interest in the subject. I have a theory that people have names that suit their characters. Call it a hobby of mine."

"I thought your hobby was train-spotting," said Lionel, and was gratified when the man responded by saying he was quick on the uptake.

Lionel put away his notebook and said, "I'll tell you my name, but I won't say if it's my real one or not."

"Fair enough," said the man, with a smile.

"Lionel Blake."

"I'm Anthony Vowels. Glad to make your acquaintance, Lionel."

Lionel had no alternative but to shake the man's hand. It was dry and hot. He wondered if Mr Vowels was aware of the other man with the same tie sitting just a few feet away from him, but as he had his back to that part of the coach it seemed unlikely. Did the stout man think Mr Vowels was following him? Were they enemies or conspirators? A mystery already! Lionel grew more and more thrilled as he watched the passing scenery and realised that he was entirely on his own in this, miles from anyone he knew. A lone wolf!

The young man awoke and looked out of the window. Then he turned to Mr Vowels and asked anxiously, "Where are we? We haven't passed Oxford yet, have we?"

"Not yet," replied Mr Vowels, looking happy about the young man's return to a waking state. He was obviously a man who liked to enliven his journeys with conversation, for he was soon chatting to the young man as if he had known him all his life, and Lionel was temporarily forgotten.

Lionel stood up and went along the aisle, passing the stout man, who was leaning back with his eyes closed. There was no doubt about it – the ties were exactly alike. He walked on, out of the carriage and into the next, and then the next. He wanted to tell all those people who smiled at him that they needn't think he was a stranger to this sort of thing, that he was quite used to travelling about on his own, but he contented himself instead with a few mysterious looks.

He found the buffet car and bought a drink of lemonade with some of the money that Linnet had given him. He had just finished drinking when somebody said they were coming into Oxford. Perhaps it would be as well to go back to his seat in case it was taken by a passenger boarding there. When he got back he saw that the young man had already made his way to the nearest exit and that Mr Vowels was sitting in his vacated seat. The lady was just leaving, too.

Mr Vowels started to talk again. He was telling him about the famous university at Oxford. Lionel didn't divulge the information that his parents had studied there. He was glad when a steward came along to say that lunch was being served. Mr Vowels prepared to leave. "Are you taking lunch, Lionel?" he asked.

"No, I brought sandwiches."

"I'll see you later, then. You can read my

newspaper if you like."

"Thanks."

Mr Vowels was easing himself out of his seat when the stout man came by. They recognised each other in the same instant. What Lionel found most interesting about the encounter was that neither of them looked particularly pleased to see the other. Mr Vowels said, "Knight! I didn't know you were coming on this train!"

"I don't suppose you did," was the response, accompanied by a dry little smile.

"Where are you off to?"

"Visiting my grandmother." But it was obvious by the way he said it that that wasn't so. They went out towards the restaurant car.

Lionel ate his sandwiches and then pretended to read the newspaper. He watched the scenery. He made some notes. It seemed a long time before the two men came back from lunch. Lionel had already thought about the possibility that Mr Knight would take the vacant seat next to Mr Vowels, so he pretended to be asleep. Maybe that way they would talk freely and might say something they wouldn't if they thought Lionel was listening.

"Hullo!" said Mr Vowels. "My enigmatic young friend has gone to sleep. Travelling on his own, you see, and rather wary of strangers."

"Quite right, too," was the response. "You meet some peculiar people on trains these days."

They both laughed. To Lionel's annoyance most of their conversation was conducted in voices too low to hear, but now and then he caught snatches of conversation. For a time they made little sense, until Mr Vowels said, "Look here, Knight, I got on to him first ..."

The reply was muffled as the train plunged into a tunnel, then the words, "Baker tried before."

"... been after him for years and this time I mean to get him."

"... get the gold, whatever it costs."

Lionel's blood seemed to curdle. He kept his eyes tightly shut and strained his ears to catch more. They were actually planning a murder!

"... no description ... know what he looks like ... Baker knows him ..."

"... only one decent hotel in Dearmouth ...

have to put up with me."

". . . keep out of my way."

". . . get him first."

After a while there was silence between them, almost as if they had quarrelled. Lionel squinted through half-closed eyes and saw that Mr Vowels had taken up his newspaper again and that Mr Knight was looking out of the window. Lionel decided that he didn't like Mr Knight. He had funny ears. He wasn't surprised that he was a crook, with ears like that.

Why had they stopped talking to each other? Mr Vowels had been anxious enough to talk before. Who was it they were planning to 'get'? Why did Mr Knight look so sulky? Lionel shifted his gaze and saw with horror that Mr Vowels was looking at him over the top of his newspaper. Did he realise that Lionel had over-heard part of their conversation? Did he think he had heard it all?

He must be brave. He opened his eyes fully and stared right back at Mr Vowels, who said, "Feel better? Didn't get much sleep last night, I expect, for excitement?"

Lionel affected a sudden deafness so that Mr Vowels might think he hadn't heard a thing, and asked him to repeat the question. Mr Vowels only smiled, glanced sideways at the other man, and returned to his newspaper.

Chapter Three

UNCLE Richard was tall, rather shabby, good-natured, and very understanding of young people. He greeted Lionel as if they had parted only yesterday and didn't ask him how his mother was, or say that he'd grown, or ask how he was getting on at school. He didn't even offer to carry Lionel's suitcase for him, although Lionel was staggering under its weight. (He had put in a few crime books at the last minute in case he needed to look anything up.)

"Did you have a good journey?"

"Yes, thanks." There was a pause, then Lionel said, "I heard two men plotting a murder."

"Did you, by jove!" said Uncle Richard. "Now why doesn't that sort of thing ever happen to me on trains? I usually get lumbered with a talkative woman or a chap with a pet subject. The last time I went up to London it was a chiropodist. My feet were burning with embarrassment by the time we got to Paddington. Well, what did these two men say exactly?"

Lionel quickly gave him the gist of it.

"Where are they now?"

"Right behind us. One is carrying a raincoat. His name's Mr Vowels, and the other one with him is Mr Knight."

Uncle Richard frowned. "Vowels," he said. "Now where have I heard that name before? Lots of Knights, of course." They walked on towards the ticket barrier. "I'll turn round casually and have a look when we pass into the booking hall."

In the booking hall Lionel pretended to transfer his suitcase from one hand to the other so as to give Uncle Richard an opportunity of glancing backwards. "Well?" he asked breathlessly. "Do you know them?"

"Can't say I do. I must say, they don't look very desperate to me, but you never can tell. You're quite sure they mentioned gold and 'getting' someone?"

"Oh yes! And they mentioned somebody called Baker."

"Baker!" Uncle Richard said it in a different sort of voice from the one he had been using, as if he were surprised.

"Yes, do you know somebody called Baker?"

"I met someone of that name, years ago, but there again, it's quite common." He walked over to the bookstall and bought a magazine. Mr Knight and Mr Vowels passed, nodding to Lionel and glancing casually at Uncle Richard. They showed no further interest and went out through the doors.

"Do you think we ought to tell the police?" Lionel whispered to Uncle Richard.

"Oh no," was the amazing response, "no fun in that. Let's follow them and see where they go."

Lionel was speechless. He had always known that Uncle Richard was a man who sometimes enjoyed playing pranks, but this was beyond his wildest dreams! Even Dad wouldn't have entered into the spirit of the thing with so much enthusiasm.

"They're going for a cab," said Uncle Richard. "Come on, my car's just over there. Keep your eyes skinned and let me know where they go. Here, let me take that suitcase – save time."

Lionel surrendered the suitcase. He followed Uncle Richard, and a few moments later they were following the cab through the centre of the town. It was the most gloriously exciting thing that Lionel had ever done. His eyes were glued to the back of the cab. He sat forward in his seat and kept repeating, "There they go. Don't lose them, Uncle Richard!" How glad he was that he hadn't gone to Newcastle with Grandpa! Compared with this, how dull it would have been sitting in Aunt Essie's spotless sitting-room, being taken to places he didn't really want to see, or being shown off to friends of Aunt Essie's who wanted to meet the son of the famous anthropologists, Lionel and Christina Blake.

After a few minutes' skilful driving, keeping well back to avoid suspicion, Uncle Richard said, "I think they must be making for The Silver Cliffs Hotel."

"Is that far?"

"Just around the next bend. It's the only hotel along this road, so, unless they're going to stay with friends in one of the houses along there, it must be The Silver Cliffs."

"No, it's the hotel. One of them did mention it. I don't know why they're both staying in the same place. I don't think they were a bit pleased to see each other."

"That's interesting," said Uncle Richard.

He pulled in to the side of the road as the cab turned into an opening between two high walls.

"Can't we follow them in there?" asked Lionel.

"I think it would be best not to. I think I'd better take you home."

"Oh, Uncle Richard, no!"

"But we'll come back," promised Uncle Richard, smiling. "We'll have tea at the hotel. The Silver Cliffs runs some rather amusing tea dances in the conservatory, and as I supply the plants for the hotel I'm very well known there. What more natural than that I should bring my nephew to see the place? I think it's quite likely that your two acquaintances will join the other guests at the tea dance. Nobody misses out on that – it's one of the hotel's specialities."

It seemed such a sensible idea that Lionel agreed to the plan, begging only that they should wait until the empty cab returned, so that they would know the two men had been deposited at the hotel. A few minutes afterwards the cab headed back towards town. It was unoccupied except for the driver, who took no interest in Lionel and Uncle Richard as he drove past.

"No suspicion there, at any rate," Uncle Richard said cheerfully. "Your two acquaintances from the train might be a little surprised when you turn up at the hotel for tea, but we'll deal with that easily enough. Come on, let's go home. I'll show you my African violets."

Uncle Richard's house was set in several cres of land, much of it occupied by the huge glasshouses in which he grew his plants. Lionel had often heard his parents talk about Uncle Richard's success. He had green fingers, they said, and anything he touched seemed to flourish. He had started in a small way by selling house plants in the local shops and the Saturday open-air market, and gradually his reputation had spread until he was now supplying plants to famous country houses, royal residences, and the homes of many famous people. He supplied flowers to decorate concert halls and churches, and ballerinas and opera singers had received his bouquets on stage. It was all very pleasant, no doubt, but Lionel had always felt that Uncle Richard ought to have been doing something far more dashing and adventurous. Sometimes he wondered what Uncle Richard had done before that, when he had lived with Aunt Maria in London.

His business was called Blooms, and most people in Dearmouth were under the impression that that was his name. On his last visit to Lionel's house he had laughed about it and said he never corrected the mistake. Lionel remembered that particularly because he quite liked the idea of his uncle having an assumed name: it gave him an extra charm in Lionel's eyes.

Uncle Richard's housekeeper, Mrs Carrington, greeted Lionel with her customary mixture of sternness and pleasure. She was an elderly lady who had something wrong with one foot, so that she limped a little, but she was otherwise quite active, and fond of sporting personalities.

"Well, young man," she said, "have you joined a sports club yet?"

Lionel had to admit that he hadn't.

"Shame on you, a young, healthy boy like you, able to run and jump and spring about as you please. Don't you know how fortunate you are?"

"Yes, Mrs Carrington."

"Here am I, a cripple from birth, who would

have loved more than anything else in the world
to be an athlete, whilst you, as perfect a picture
of health as I ever saw, don't play games at all."

"I play football at school, Mrs Carrington."
He didn't say he hated it.

Uncle Richard said, "Lionel is mentally ath-
letic, Carrie. Don't pretend to be so cross. We
know you aren't."

"Well, it seems unnatural to me that a healthy
boy like Lionel doesn't want to compete in
sporting activities." But she smiled as she said
it.

"I prefer to do things on my own, Mrs Carrington," said Lionel. "I'm a lone wolf, like
Uncle Richard."

Uncle Richard laughed, but Mrs Carrington
looked astonished and said what an old head
he had on his young shoulders, which rather
pleased Lionel. She had proved her true nature
by providing all the things that had pleased him
on his last visit, eighteen months before. His
favourite books were on the bedside table in his
room under the eaves, a bowl of nuts and fruit
on the dressing table, the old concertina lying

on the chair. Downstairs it was the same, his favourite dishes prepared in the kitchen and black grapes on the sideboard. The best thing of all was that she didn't tell him to change into indoor shoes, she didn't tell him to keep his hands off the polished furniture. He smiled his thanks to her and she rumpled his hair and said he was a charmer just like his uncle.

He could hardly wait to get back to the hotel, but he dutifully drank the milk shake he was offered and then went with Uncle Richard to look at the glasshouses. There were girls working in them and they smiled and would have kept him talking, but he reminded Uncle Richard that they were going out to tea. He didn't want him to change his mind about it. Grown-up people often had second thoughts about things like that, but Uncle Richard said, "Yes, let's go."

They went back to the house to change into clean shirts. Uncle Richard said they must wear ties because it was a house rule at The Silver Cliffs. That reminded Lionel of the ties which the two men on the train had been wearing.

"Did you notice," he asked his uncle, "that the two men were wearing the same college tie?"

"No, I didn't notice that. Maybe that explains it all. It might be a college rag they're planning – a reunion prank."

"It didn't sound like that. I can't explain it properly because you didn't hear it, but the way they said what they did say sounded – sinister."

"Oh dear, you're making my blood run cold."

As they got into the car Uncle Richard asked him what else he could remember about the two men. "Well," said Lionel, "I don't think they know what the man looks like."

"What man?"

"The one they're going to kill. And they seemed to be having an argument as to which one of them was going to do it. They both wanted to. They both wanted to be the one to get the gold."

"Are you quite sure of all this, Lionel?"

"Yes." He watched Uncle Richard as he drove out of the lane into the main stream of traffic going into Dearmouth. "You know what I'm going to be when I grow up?"

"Tell me."

"A private investigator. A detective. But they don't take me seriously at home. They never do. Do you think it's a stupid ambition, Uncle Richard? Linnet does."

"Not a bit. Just the sort of thing I'd have liked to have been."

"Honestly?"

"Why not? Lots of men fancy themselves as super-heroes. Most of us change our minds as we get older and become nurserymen or accountants or shopkeepers – something safe and profitable – but that's no reason for stifling a secret longing for a life of action." He glanced at Lionel. "I'll let you into a secret."

"Yes?" said Lionel breathlessly.

"I already knew about your ambition."

"How?"

"Your mother told me about it on the phone yesterday."

Lionel, who had thought for a moment that Uncle Richard was going to reveal something exciting about his secret life, snorted with indignation and disappointment. "You don't think

I'm making it all up, do you? I mean, the men on the train and everything?"

"Why should I think that?"

"Because of what Mum said."

"Of course not. Don't spoil everything. I haven't had this much fun in years."

"Do you mean that?"

"Of course I do."

Lionel seemed to ride on a cloud all the way to the hotel.

The conservatory in which the tea dances were held was a large construction of wrought-iron and glass, built on to the back of the hotel. It contained hundreds of potted plants and a huge grape-vine. It had been built at the request of a royal visitor to the town at the turn of the century, and a plaque on the wall outside bore the information that that same regal personage had laid the foundation stone in 1907. Tea dances had been held there ever since. Fashions might change, people might come and go, but The Silver Cliffs tea dances went on. The orchestra still played the same old tunes on the same little dais, the waiters moved discreetly among the tables, some of them appearing so old that they might have been the original ones who had served His Royal Highness.

"Of course it's outrageously expensive to maintain these days," Uncle Richard said as they approached, "but every time there is a suggestion that the tea dances should be discontinued, there is a public outcry and people get up petitions to keep them going. It's become such a tradition that visitors come from all over the world to sample this quaint custom."

A waiter approached them as they entered. "Good afternoon, Mr Bloom. A table for two?"

"Yes please, John."

Lionel whispered, "He called you Mr Bloom."

"Yes, they all do. I never discourage them. It's good for business, you see."

Although Lionel didn't see why Richard Flaxby of Blooms Nurseries shouldn't be equally good for business, he had to admit that he didn't know much about such things, so he stayed silent. When they were seated Uncle Richard said, with a twinkle in his eyes, "I rather enjoy the feeling of being incognito. I think it gives me an air of mystery. You see, your mother is quite right when she says I haven't completely grown up yet."

"Linnet's just the same about me."

Lionel looked around the room. There was no sign of the two men. He was disappointed, but he tried to listen to Uncle Richard when he started to tell him about the different flowers and plants. The waiter brought tea, toasted tea cakes and cream cakes, and then moved away as someone else entered the conservatory. It was Mr Vowels.

Lionel exchanged a glance with Uncle Richard, who calmly began to pour the tea. The waiter conducted Mr Vowels to the vacant table next to theirs. He smiled when he saw Lionel. "We meet again," he said, nodding affably at Uncle Richard. Then, as he sat down, he began to talk to the waiter about the flowers, and the waiter murmured something to him, glancing at Uncle Richard as he bent over.

"Excuse me, Mr Bloom," the waiter said, "I've just been telling this gentleman that you are the one who is responsible for the floral decor. I hope you don't mind?"

"Not at all," smiled Uncle Richard.

"A credit to you, Mr Bloom," said Mr Vowels.

"Thank you."

Mr Vowels' bland expression suddenly changed. He scowled a little. Lionel followed the direction of his glance and saw that Mr Knight was entering. He came over to Mr Vowels' table and said, "Pax for now, old man – you don't mind if I join you, do you?"

"For the time being, no."

Lionel concentrated on eating his cake with a fork instead of biting into it as he would have done at home, and he was obliged to listen to what Uncle Richard was telling him about the way his business had grown. It was all very interesting, no doubt, but he desperately wanted to hear instead what the two men at the next table were saying.

After some time Mr Knight left the table saying something about a phone call. Mr Vowels watched him go with a thoughtful and somewhat cunning expression on his face. When Mr Knight had disappeared, he leaned over towards Uncle Richard and said, "Pardon me, Mr Bloom, but as you are a man of business in the town I think you may be able to help me."

Uncle Richard met his look with admirable calm. "Indeed?" he said.

"Yes. You see, I'm trying to trace someone – an old friend, an old school friend – and although my information is that he is resident in Dearmouth he doesn't seem to be listed in the telephone directory."

"So how can I help you?"

"Well, it occurs to me, that as you come in contact with most of the residents here, you might have heard something of my old friend." He stopped for a moment, but as Uncle Richard remained silent, he went on, "It's just that I should like to see him again, chat over old times and so forth, have dinner together, you understand?"

"Perfectly," agreed Uncle Richard. "What is his name?"

With a glance at the door as if to make sure

that his friend wasn't returning, Mr Vowels
leaned further forward and said in a whisper,
"His name is Richard Flaxby."

Chapter Four

"BUT don't you see, Uncle Richard, it's *you* they're after. What are you going to do? Are you going to tell the police?"

Lionel was trying hard to keep pace with his uncle as he strode over towards his car, but every now and then he had to give a little hop, skip, and jump, and that made him angry. One of these days he'd be as tall and as broad as Uncle Richard and then he wouldn't worry about people wanting to bump him off, but for the moment his chief worry was that Mr Knight was lying in wait for them somewhere.

"When they find out who you really are," he gasped, "they'll be very angry."

"They won't find out," smiled Uncle Richard, "not after what I told Mr Vowels."

"That Richard Flaxby used to live in Dearmouth but that he went to farm sheep in Australia? Do you think he believed you?"

"No reason why he shouldn't. I thought I was very convincing."

As they drove away Lionel asked, "Did you know them? Was Mr Vowels really at school with you?"

"Certainly not." Uncle Richard put on an exaggerated manner. "Type like that wouldn't be allowed over the threshold at my old school. Dreadful taste in ties."

"That's the tie I told you about. Mr Knight's wearing one exactly the same."

"So I noticed. Did you ever see anything so hideous?"

"Are we being followed?"

"No." He looked amazingly calm. "Don't you think you ought to be treating all this with a little more sang-froid, old chap?"

"What's that?"

"Composure. Coolness. After all, if you're going to be a detective – sorry, private investigator – you'll have to stop panicking about situations of this sort."

Lionel leaned back in his seat. Uncle Richard was quite right. He pondered the facts so far. "I think you know something you're not telling me," he said.

"Well done," responded Uncle Richard softly.

"I think you do know those two men."

"I never saw them before in my life."

"But you know who they are."

"I have my suspicions as to who they are, and I don't want them to know who I am, but for the moment that's all I'm going to say."

"Oh, Uncle Richard, you . . ."

"You want to be a detective?"

"You know I do."

"Very well, then, detect. Do your stuff. See

if you can solve this mystery entirely on your own. Then you'll have somebody to back up your ambition."

"You mean you'd be on my side? You'd tell them at home that I *could* be a P.I.? That it's not just kids' stuff?"

"Certainly."

"I'll do it," said Lionel.

Uncle Richard just nodded and then became preoccupied with his own thoughts. Lionel wondered what they were. What were the problems that Grandpa had spoken of? Who were those two men, and why were they out to get Uncle Richard? It was all very well for him to take the matter so calmly, but *he* hadn't heard the conversation on the train, *he* hadn't seen the look of annoyance on the two men's faces when they had encountered each other. Sitting in the conservatory drinking tea they had both looked the picture of innocence, but had Uncle Richard quite understood why Mr Vowels had waited until his companion had left the room before putting his questions to him? Was he really as unconcerned as he appeared, or was he putting on a brave face for Lionel's benefit?

Well, Uncle Richard had been warned, and if he chose to ignore the warning that was his lookout. Lionel would find out what was going on. He would keep an eye on things. After all, he was a lone wolf, wasn't he? He could manage this thing without help.

Maybe Uncle Richard was fobbing him off about solving the mystery on his own – because he knew that he wouldn't be able to do it. That was like most grown-up people, but he had never thought it of Uncle Richard. He had always seemed to understand. There had been that super Christmas when he had organised a treasure hunt for Christmas presents instead of putting them under the tree like everybody else. There had been the wonderful day when he had taken Lionel across the water to the uninhabited island – a bird sanctuary, it was called – and they had found footprints in the sand, just like Robinson Crusoe. They had followed them, and somehow it hadn't mattered that the man had turned out to be a wildlife warden and one of Uncle Richard's friends. What mattered about

Uncle Richard's schemes was that at the time you believed in them.

As they got out of the car Uncle Richard told Lionel not to say anything to Mrs Carrington about the two men. It might frighten her, he said. Lionel nodded sagely, but kept to himself his intention of asking her a few questions. He must think carefully about the best way of putting them, so he went upstairs and lay down on the bed. He was sure he hadn't slept, but it was almost time for supper when he looked at the clock. He went downstairs carrying the gift for Uncle Richard and the box of chocolates that Mum had sent for Mrs Carrington. They were both very pleased.

"We've been having a chat about what we're going to do with you," said Mrs Carrington. "We must organise some outings."

Lionel gave Uncle Richard a quick glance. "I've got lots of things to do," he said.

"Such as?" enquired Mrs Carrington.

"Walking," said Lionel. "Going into town and looking around."

"I should think there are far better things

for a boy of your age to be doing," cried Mrs Carrington. "Now tomorrow there's a tennis tournament starting at The Silver Cliffs courts. I'd already booked two tickets, one for myself and one for your uncle, but he's agreed that you can go in his place."

Uncle Richard was looking down at his plate. Lionel realised that the tennis courts in question were those he had noticed when they had driven to the hotel. Was that why Uncle Richard had given up his place? Did he think it was a good opportunity for Lionel to go and have a look at what Mr Vowels and Mr Knight were doing? "All right, Mrs Carrington," he said. "I'll come with you."

"Good," she said. "And we're all going to the theatre tomorrow night. You'd like that, wouldn't you?"

Lionel was more cautious about that. "It isn't ballet or anything, is it?" he asked.

Uncle Richard looked up and laughed. "As a matter of fact," he said, "it's right up your street – an Agatha Christie mystery."

"Great!" shouted Lionel.

When the meal was over Uncle Richard suggested that he should ring home to let them know he had arrived safely and was settled in. It was Dad who answered the phone. "Hullo, Dad," he said, "I've arrived."

"Good. Doing anything exciting?"

Lionel hesitated, then said, "I'm going to a tennis tournament tomorrow and the theatre tomorrow night."

"Excellent. I'm glad you're getting a bit of culture. No problems I suppose?"

"No."

"How was the journey?"

"Fine. Nothing to it."

They talked about the weather and about Linnet going off to stay with Amanda; a few quick words with Mum about changing his socks every day (she had already said all that before he left) and not eating bananas because they disagreed with him, and he was once more the lone wolf. He was getting into his pyjamas when Mrs Carrington called upstairs to tell him that Grandpa was on the phone.

He hurried downstairs. "Hullo, Grandpa.

Are you having a good time? I am."

"I'm very glad to hear it. Not making you change your trousers before you come into the house are they?"

"No. Why?"

"Aunt Essie makes me do it. She's had a place built on at the back where Jim and I have to take our oily trousers off – she *says* they must be oily because we're working in them, but they're not that bad – and she won't let us in the house until we've done it. She never allows anybody to come in by the front door because they might soil her doorstep. And I've got to fold all my clothes, even in my own room, and not make a mess with the soap . . ."

"With the soap?"

"Yes, I've got to rinse the soap when I've finished with it. Did you ever hear anything like it? Poor old Jim – she treats his customers with the greatest suspicion. She never did like strangers, but if they're dressed in anything out of the ordinary she's convinced they've come to mess up her house."

"Poor Grandpa!"

"I'm glad I didn't insist on bringing you with me. Are you okay?"

"Oh yes!"

"I've got one consolation, though. When I'm in the workshop it's a different world. Oh, you should see it! All the latest equipment, bang up to the minute, and all the bike enthusiasts for miles around come here. It's a kind of meeting place. I've had a lot of fun already talking to them. So don't get the impression that I'm miserable all the time." He rattled on for a while. All the time Lionel was bursting to ask him a question.

At last, when he paused for breath, Lionel lowered his voice and said, "Grandpa, I want to ask you something."

"Eh? Speak up, the line's gone faint."

"A question, Grandpa. I want to ..." He broke off. Uncle Richard had crossed the hall and was doing something within earshot. "Oh, it doesn't matter."

"What is it, Lionel? Something bothering you?"

"No."

"You are happy there, aren't you?"

"Yes."

"Well, don't forget to send me a postcard. You remember your aunt's address, don't you? Mrs Shipstocks, Main Street ..."

"Yes, I remember, Grandpa."

He hung up and went to bed. He would send Grandpa a postcard view of Dearmouth. He'd like that. But it was no use bothering him about the question. He'd have to find out about that on his own.

His last thoughts before he fell asleep were very muddled. Mr Knight and Mr Vowels seemed to be riding motorbikes around the tennis court. Aunt Essie was pursuing them with a duster. Grandpa was playing tennis with Mrs Carrington ... poor Grandpa. Aunt Essie had no right to treat him the way she did. One day Lionel would get even with her for the things she was making Grandpa do ...

Chapter Five

THE following day dawned bright and cloud-less. Uncle Richard had breakfasted early so as to be in the glasshouses for a few hours before going off to make his business calls, so Lionel took the opportunity of asking Mrs Carrington those questions he had thought of. He started by asking if the knife and fork he was using were made of real silver. Mrs Carrington said they were plated. He then said he supposed some people used real gold cutlery, and she said she supposed some people might, but she'd never been in that sort of company.

"Has Uncle Richard got any gold?" he asked.

"Gold? He has a gold watch, I believe."

"Is he rich?"

"Heaven bless the boy! What questions you do ask! I can't answer that. You'll have to ask your uncle."

"He's not poor though, is he? I suppose he might have some gold."

"Well, if he has I haven't seen it."

"Do you think anybody might want to rob him?"

"Oh, that's what you're afraid of! Well, that's natural enough, I suppose, being away from home and sleeping in a strange house, but there's no need to bother your head about that. We're secure enough here. We lock up tightly every night. Besides, Mr Richard never was one to fill his house with expensive things. No antiques or original paintings or anything of that sort. He prefers plain, ordinary things about him. So don't worry your head about burglars. There are far better pickings to be had in Dearmouth than what we've got here."

She seemed to think she had answered his questions to his complete satisfaction, for immediately afterwards she got up and said she was going into the garden to make sure there was some salad for supper.

Lionel went into the sitting room to look at Uncle Richard's tropical fish, which he kept in a large tank fixed to the wall. There were lots of new ones since Lionel had been there before – some beautiful black ones – and Lionel spent quite a long time watching them swimming through the special oxygenating plants and ornamental rocks. His mind was full of the mystery, however. He still hadn't made up his mind whether Uncle Richard was hiding a terrible secret from him or whether he genuinely believed that the two men were harmless, but either way Lionel felt that he wasn't taking the threat as seriously as he ought to be. Why was he so anxious that they shouldn't know his real name?

Where did the truth lie? Was it somewhere in

Uncle Richard's past? He tried to recall everything that Mum had told him about when Uncle Richard worked in London, but all he could remember was that he had gone to an office every day, nine to five, and had a very good position. Then, she had said, when Aunt Maria died, he had suddenly decided to change his life-style completely and, seeing a small market garden advertised for sale in Dearmouth, he had bought it and turned it over to flower growing. Everybody had said it would never work, but it had. That was all.

Lionel went to the door. As he passed a small table (on which he sometimes played chess with Uncle Richard) his eyes were caught by a book lying there. It was a large, paper-covered book, like a scrap book. It hadn't been there the previous night, and Lionel was idly curious as to why it was there now. He took a closer look at it. It seemed to be a kind of scrap book of newspaper cuttings and photographs, all old, and rather worn. When he looked at the first page he thought he knew why Uncle Richard had taken it out. He was going to show it to

Lionel because it was all about Grandfather Flaxby – Mum's and Uncle Richard's father, whom Lionel had never known.

He turned over the pages. The whole book seemed to be devoted to the subject of soccer. There were team photographs, old match programmes, entrance tickets to football grounds, accounts of matches held long ago. He noticed that all the cuttings related to one particular team called Wytcham United, and a closer inspection told Lionel that Grandfather Flaxby had been the manager of that team. That was something that nobody had ever told Lionel. Maybe if he had known that he might have thought about football with different feelings.

He was just closing the book when his attention was caught by a picture on the back page. Apparently Wytcham United had won a cup. The photograph showed the victorious team posing with the cup, and underneath was the date of the final, May 10th, 1948. That was a coincidence – it was Uncle Richard's birthday. He remembered that because Linnet's birthday was the 11th and he always had to buy two birthday cards at the same time.

Grandfather Flaxby was in the picture too, a large, happy, smiling man, undoubtedly very proud of his team. Someone – probably Grandfather Flaxby – had written out in pencil underneath the photograph the names of the members of the winning team, not once, but several times, all in different orders. It was funny the way he had done that, and Lionel didn't close the book until he had thought of an explanation for it. Grandfather Flaxby had been working out the positions of the team for a future match. Lionel always played a midfield position, but occasionally had been in goal. He wondered what Grandfather Flaxby would have done with him. He closed the book and soon forgot it.

Later, Mrs Carrington came downstairs ready to go. "I've packed a picnic lunch," she said brightly, "and we'll be home in time for tea. I'm sure you're going to enjoy it just as much as I am. I go to all the tournaments and I always enjoy them."

Mrs Carrington rode in the front seat beside Uncle Richard and Lionel went in the back.

There had been no opportunity to discuss the mystery, and Lionel wondered if Uncle Richard had forgotten about it. He chatted to Mrs Carrington in his normal cheerful manner, every now and then throwing a word or two to Lionel in the back.

It was when they had stopped at traffic lights in the town that Lionel spotted Mr Vowels and Mr Knight. They were not together. Mr Vowels was hurrying along the street alone – but the strange thing was that Mr Knight seemed to be tailing him! He kept close to the shop windows, every now and then slipping into a doorway to avoid observation. Lionel looked at the back of Uncle Richard's head, but if he had recognised, or even seen the two men, he gave no sign of it. He was whistling to himself.

How Lionel would have loved to jump out and follow them! But just then the lights changed and Uncle Richard drove on. He dropped Lionel and Mrs Carrington outside the hotel and told them he would be back to take them home at 5 o'clock. Mrs Carrington led the way to the tennis court and took her seat. She appeared to be very well-known there for lots of people spoke to her. Lionel found himself sitting between her and a jolly little man with black eyes who began to talk to Lionel as if he had known him all his life. After a while Lionel glanced at Mrs Carrington. She had placed an inflatable cushion behind her head (they were on the back row, against the boards) and was fast asleep.

"Gone off has she?" smiled the little man.

Lionel said she was asleep, if that was what he meant.

"That's it, son. Regular as clockwork, that is. I think it must be the buff-buff of the ball that sends her off, every time. Sleeps right through it, except for a snack at lunch, and then says what a good match it's been and how much she's enjoyed it. Well, maybe she has. Who's to blame her? Though it does seem to me she could do that in her own garden without going to the expense of buying tickets. Well –" He stood up. "I have to go now. I help in the dressing rooms, you see. Enjoy the match."

"Thanks," said Lionel.

He was pleased with the way things had worked out. Now he could go to the hotel and have a look around without anybody being any the wiser. There were lots of people about and nobody would bother about a boy who might be staying in the hotel. Very cautiously he raised himself from his seat. Mrs Carrington was gently snoring, her hat pulled right down over her eyes. She had brought with her a long woollen scarf in case the weather turned chilly, but there was little likelihood of that now, for the sun was quite hot. Lionel took it out of the bag and wound it around his neck and chin. Then he put on the woolly hat and pulled it well down over his ears. Finally he put on Mum's old sunglasses. He felt that he could have done better given more time for preparation, but it wasn't a bad disguise.

The tennis courts were connected to the hotel grounds by a broad gravel walk leading to a flight of stone steps. Lionel hurried along the walk and joined in behind a party of several people who were going in the direction of the hotel. He followed them right into the foyer, where they took the lift and left him alone. He took a seat in an alcove where he was concealed from general view by a sort of trellis and an arrangement of potted plants (Uncle Richard's, he thought), and waited for something to happen. Lionel believed in taking things as they came.

He had been there for about ten minutes when Mr Vowels came hurrying into the foyer, mopping his brow as if he had been hurrying. There was a grin on his face. He didn't take the lift but went upstairs two at a time. Shortly afterwards Mr Knight came puffing through the revolving doors. He too took the stairs.

Lionel waited. A man who had the appearance of being in authority asked Lionel if he was waiting for someone.

"Yes," responded Lionel quite truthfully, "Mr Vowels."

"Ah yes, Mr Vowels. Shall I tell him that you are waiting to see him?"

"No, I'll just wait."

"Don't you find it a little too warm wrapped up like that?"

"No – I've got mumps."

"Dear me – should you be out?" The man stepped back a pace or two.

"I'm okay. It doesn't hurt much."

The man gave him a strange look and went along the corridor. Lionel felt quite pleased with himself. He had noticed before that you had only to mention things like measles and mumps for people to back off. He was learning fast how to think quickly in a difficult situation.

About five minutes later Mr Vowels came down wearing a fresh shirt but with the same tie. Evidently he was very attached to it, for it didn't blend with his shirt at all. Lionel crouched low and peered at him through the trellis. He was looking at some advertisements on the desk. He turned to go in the direction of the dining room. At that moment Mr Knight came running heavily down the stairs. When he saw Mr Vowels he gave rather a sheepish grin.

"No need to hurry, old man," chortled Mr Vowels, "I'm only going in to lunch."

Mr Knight looked quite put out. "Why don't you give up?" he said.

"Why should I be the one to give up? I got on to him first. And judging by your complete lack of initiative this morning I don't have much to worry about." His chortle became a laugh. "What a dance I led you! I haven't enjoyed anything so much for years. Pack it in, old man, can't outwit an old fox like me."

Mr Knight snapped, "We'll see about that. I mean to get Flaxby and I don't care what it costs." And he walked into the dining room. Mr Vowels followed him. Lionel noticed that they sat at separate tables.

He went out through the revolving doors and found his way to the steps. He walked slowly. He He was more than ever convinced that Uncle Richard hadn't realised that these men were in deadly earnest. A lady passed him on the steps. She was tall and stern-looking and she gave Lionel a nod as she passed. He had gone only a few paces more when he noticed a scarf lying on the gravel walk and his heart quickened as he bent to pick it up. It was the same colour and bore the same motif as the ties worn by Mr Vowels and Mr Knight! She was another member of the gang!

A hand fell on his shoulder and a silky voice said, "Well, Lionel?"

Chapter Six

LIONEL turned and looked up into the face of
Mr Vowels.

"I was told that you wanted to see me,
Lionel."

Lionel slipped the hand holding the scarf
behind his back. If they knew that he was on to
them they might become really desperate, so
although he trembled, he stood his ground.

"I thought I'd come back later," he said,

"when you'd finished your lunch." If ever he had needed to be quick-witted he needed to be now!

"What did you want to see me about?"

"I – I had a message from my uncle."

"From Mr Bloom? Well?"

"He remembered something about Richard Flaxby."

"Yes?" said Mr Vowels eagerly, too eagerly for Lionel's liking.

"He says that when Richard Flaxby went to Australia he took all his – all his valuables with him. He needed all his money and all his – gold – and everything – to buy the sheep."

Mr Vowels frowned. "Well, I suppose he would," he said. "Tell your uncle that I sent off a cable to that address in Australia he gave me, but that I haven't had a reply yet. Oh, and I'd rather you didn't mention anything about the Australian business to anybody else, particularly my friend Mr Knight, who seems determined to – to forestall me in a certain matter. Do you understand?"

"Yes."

Mr Vowels was turning to go when he suddenly said, "What's that you've got there?"

"Got where?"

"That scarf?"

"It's Mrs Carrington's. She's my uncle's housekeeper and she's quite old. She gets very cold sometimes, so she always takes a woolly scarf with her in case the weather turns cold."

"Not that scarf. The other one."

"Oh!" said Lionel, as if he had forgotten that he had it. "Oh, I just found it."

"Where?"

"Here."

"On this spot, you mean?"

"Yes, I think it must belong to the lady who just passed me."

"A lady passed you? I didn't see anyone."

"She could have gone through the conservatory."

"Yes, she could. Describe her."

"She was tall and strong-looking, quite stern."

"Short grey hair? Dressed in tweeds?"

"Yes."

Mr Vowels' brow darkened. He held out his hand for the scarf. Lionel had no alternative but to hand it over.

"Baker," muttered Mr Vowels to himself, "of all people it had to be Baker." He pulled himself together and smiled again at Lionel. "Don't worry about the scarf," he said. "I'll return it. But remember, not a word to anyone – anyone, you understand?"

Lionel nodded dumbly. He was quite sure that the words contained a threat and that he was being ordered not to inform the police. The only consolation he had was that Mr Vowels still didn't seem to suspect that Uncle Richard was the man he was looking for. He stared after Mr Vowels as he puffed up the steps and disappeared in the direction of the conservatory. What a strange gang they were! They all seemed to be trying to outwit one another, not working together at all, for it was obvious that Mr Vowels had been anything but pleased to know that the lady called Baker was there in Dearmouth.

He wandered back towards the tennis courts, his thoughts tumbling over one another like clowns in a circus ring. Baker was the name he had overheard on the train. And hadn't Uncle Richard admitted that he had once met someone of that name? Wouldn't it be *awful* if it turned out that Uncle Richard had once belonged to the gang and had made off with some gold belonging to them, and now they were out to avenge themselves and recover the gold? It couldn't be – not his favourite uncle! But he *had* moved away from the place where he had lived with Aunt Maria, hadn't he? And he *did* go under the name of Bloom here, instead of Flaxby.

Lionel slipped into his seat just as Mrs Carrington woke up.

"Oh, Lionel," she said, glancing at the score board, "I must have just dozed off for a moment or two. So unlike me. I see that Angela's winning. I thought she would. Have you had a drink?" She looked at him more closely. "Do you feel unwell? You're awfully flushed."

"I'm just hot."

"I don't wonder at it with that scarf twisted around your neck like that. Surely you're not sickening for something?"

"Oh, no. I was just trying it on, that's all."
He unwound the scarf and took off the hat and
sunglasses. He supposed Mr Vowels must have
recognised his jeans and sweater, which were
the same ones he had been wearing in the train.
His heart was still thumping uncomfortably,
more from the sickening thought that Uncle
Richard had once been an associate of that gang
than from fear of Mr Vowels. He took the pasty
and the drink that Mrs Carrington handed him
out of the bag and began to feel better. After all,
if Uncle Richard had relented his past and was
trying to make amends by going straight, he
ought to help him. He would stand by him
whatever happened.

No wonder he had been too ashamed to admit
the truth to him. He must feel pretty bad about
it. All these and many other thoughts occupied
Lionel's mind during the rest of the tournament, and it was only when he saw his uncle
coming for them that he told himself that his
theory must be wrong. Uncle Richard was so
unconcerned, so pleasant, with such an honest

face – and besides, he was *Mum's brother*.

Yet – he pondered as he took a shower before supper – there could be no other explanation. Everything fitted the theory so perfectly. Why was it that in books the detective always had a brilliant idea when he was in the shower? Why didn't it happen to him? And suddenly it did.

Uncle Richard wasn't a crook at all! Lionel couldn't think where the idea came from, but he remembered hearing somewhere – maybe on TV – that some new plants were worth a fortune. Something to do with cross-pollination and a lot of luck. What if Uncle Richard had produced such a plant? A rare orchid – a gold one! The gold in question might not be the precious metal at all, but a gold-coloured flower! And these people were out to steal it, were prepared to kill for it, if necessary.

He dressed hurriedly and went into his room. There, he took out his notebook and turned his mind back to the scarf he had found. The curious combination of letters had been worked into the material of the scarf much larger than in the ties, and in his mind's eye he could see the order in which they appeared. He wrote them down: S.P.E.N. He was sure that was the correct order. With mounting excitement he realised that the S could stand for SOCIETY, and the N for NURSERYMEN, but try as he would he could think of nothing to fit the letters in between. But it was obvious now that Mr Vowels, Mr Knight, and Miss Baker were all members of a rival company who wanted to carry the new plant triumphantly away. Of course! Hadn't Mr Vowels been the one to express an interest in the plants in the conservatory? They had heard somewhere that it was Richard Flaxby who had developed the new species, and Uncle Richard knew quite well what they were after. That was why he had tried to lay a false trail by saying that Richard Flaxby had emigrated.

Feeling very pleased with himself Lionel went down to supper, which was earlier than usual on account of their intention to go to the theatre.

"You look very smug," smiled Uncle Richard.

Lionel nodded mysteriously, but held his tongue.

"I expect he's excited about the theatre," said Mrs Carrington.

Lionel exchanged a look with Uncle Richard and they seemed to perfectly understand each other. It must be wonderful to be as brave as Uncle Richard and to feel smart enough to outwit his rivals, but once again Lionel had the misgiving that his uncle didn't take his position seriously enough. Well, it was up to him to be vigilant and to warn his uncle when danger threatened more closely. He wouldn't have known they were in Dearmouth if he hadn't been alert enough to spot them.

The play was very good. Lionel followed the action with very close attention and by the end of the second act had made up his mind who the murderer was. He confided his ideas to Mrs Carrington and Uncle Richard when they went to buy a drink in the interval.

"Oh, I'm sure you're wrong, Lionel!" said Mrs Carrington. "Such a pleasant character. No, I think you're quite mistaken."

"What do you think, Uncle Richard?" asked Lionel.

Uncle Richard laughed and said he was completely baffled. He was quite sure that Lionel was far better at that sort of thing than he was. At the end of the play Lionel said, "What did I tell you?"

"You were quite right," said Mrs Carrington in some amazement, and turning to Uncle Richard she said, "Your nephew has a very devious mind, I think."

"A very sharp one, certainly," agreed Uncle Richard, putting his hand on Lionel's shoulder and squeezing it a little.

"How did you know?" Mrs Carrington wanted to know.

"It was obvious," sniffed Lionel. "The police inspector was the one whom nobody suspected, so it had to be him."

"Well I never!" said Mrs Carrington. "Fancy working it out like that!"

Lionel's mind was so keyed-up with the events of the day that he found it hard to get to sleep that night. As he tossed and turned he remembered the dark clothing and hood he had brought with him. Wouldn't it be better to settle his mind once and for all regarding the gold orchid, and then perhaps he'd be able to get to sleep?

He sat up in bed and listened. He could hear Mrs Carrington snoring next door, but there was no other sound. It would be quite easy to creep downstairs and let himself out by the back door. The orchid house was only a few steps away, along a flagged passage, so he could be there and back in just a few minutes.

He got out of bed and as quietly as he could found the dark jeans and sweater and the hood. (He dare not risk going out in his light-coloured pyjamas and dressing-gown in case the gang were out there snooping around.) He put them on quickly, then slipped his feet into the rubber shoes and went out on to the landing.

A dim light shone from underneath Uncle Richard's bedroom door. He too, it seemed, was finding sleep difficult to come by. Lionel tiptoed stealthily past. He knew which one of the stairs it was that creaked, so he stepped down two together, holding on to the banister rail, his torch tucked into the waistband of his jeans. Reaching the kitchen door in safety he found that Mrs Carrington hadn't exaggerated when she had said they locked up securely at night. There were two bolts and a lock on the door.

It seemed to take an hour to unfasten them without making a noise, but at last it was done, and Lionel stepped out into the cold night air. The faint, faraway sigh of the sea came to his ears and he could smell the salt mingling with the scent of flowers: all his senses were alert and ready to pick up the least hint of danger. He stepped out along the passageway, and shielding the torch with the palm of his hand, so that it shone red through his flesh, he approached the orchid house.

The door was padlocked! He hardly knew whether to feel frustrated or elated to know that there was something in there worth locking up, but had just decided to make a circuit of the glasshouse in search of a window which might have been left unlatched when a step behind him made his blood curdle. For the second time that day a hand fell on his shoulder. It was so like the first time that he had no doubt that when he turned he would be facing Mr Vowels, so he *didn't* turn, but stood there like a statue waiting for the next move on his assailant's part.

A quiet voice hissed, "Lionel! What on earth are you doing out here?"

The sight of Uncle Richard in his pyjamas and dressing-gown made Lionel give a slightly hysterical laugh. "Investigating," he said.

It was Uncle Richard's turn to laugh. "You are the most incredible –" he broke off and then said, "Come on, let's go and make some cocoa."

When the cocoa was made he asked, "What did you think you were going to find in the orchid house? A body?"

"Of course not. I thought you might have a rare plant in there."

Uncle Richard looked very interested. "I see. Well, they're all rather special. They have to be nurtured like delicate babies. Even opening the door on a chilly night like this could have a bad effect on them. But I haven't got anything wildly exciting."

"You haven't got a special gold one?"

"Gold?"

"I told you – the men said something about getting the gold."

"Oh yes, I remember. You know, that puzzles me too. I haven't the remotest idea what they mean by that. Cross my heart and hope to die."

"Don't say that!" said Lionel hastily, and as Uncle Richard was about to speak again, "I don't want you to tell me any more. I want to solve it all by myself."

"The lone wolf, eh?"

"That's right."

"Well, how about the lone wolf going off to his lair for a bit of shut-eye? It's terribly late. And Lionel," he went on as Lionel reached the hall door, "don't worry. There's really no need to. They're not bad people. Absolutely dotty, of course, and not the kind I want to spend my leisure time with, but not bad. Okay? Goodnight, sleep well."

Chapter Seven

IN spite of his midnight wanderings Lionel was
awake quite early the next day. He rolled over
on to his side and looked at the bookshelf over
the bed. It was quite interesting to note that
Uncle Richard must have enjoyed mystery
stories when he was a boy, because there were
all his own favourites there. Two in particular
caught his eye, *Kidnapped* and *Treasure Island*.
Lionel reached up and took them down. Idly he

opened the first one and saw Uncle Richard's name written there, in a round, schoolboy handwriting which had changed very little over the years. 'Richard Flaxby, Millford School.' Lionel flicked over the pages, remembering passages that had thrilled him on a first reading and which still made him want to read on. But he mustn't get involved. There was work to do. His very own mystery was still unsolved.

He put the book back on the shelf and picked up the other one, intending to replace it, but somehow it fell on to the bed, and when he took it up again it was open at the fly-leaf. He stared and sat back on his heels. In the same handwriting Uncle Richard had written 'Rockingstone Flaxby, Millford School.'

So *that* was what Grandpa had meant! Uncle Richard was not Uncle Richard at all, but Uncle Rockingstone. He remembered that sometimes Mum called him Rocky, but that he didn't like it. Well, Rockingstone wasn't such a bad name, was it? It was undoubtedly the sort of name that would amuse Grandpa, and Lionel couldn't help grinning a little when he recalled Grandpa's merriment. Grandpa was just plain George and proud of it.

As Lionel dressed he remembered something else. On the train Mr Vowels had said he was interested in names. Was the mystery somehow bound up with Uncle Richard's name? Just how long had his uncle called himself Richard? He had written the name Richard in one of his books, but as a schoolboy had he been known as Rockingstone – as Rocky? Did it all go back to his schooldays, as Mr Vowels had said? Lionel was halfway down the stairs when he thought of something else. Had the gang been watching *him* – Lionel – in the hope that he would eventually lead them to his uncle? What a thrilling idea!

"Coming down, Lionel?" called Mrs Carrington from the hallway, and he realised that he was standing still as a stone on the middle stair.

"Yes, coming," he replied.

He had breakfast in the kitchen with Mrs Carrington. There was a postcard from Grandpa, who must have sent it off on the night he had arrived in Newcastle. There was a picture of a bridge and a ruined castle, and Grandpa had written on the back, 'Just arrived. Miss you a lot. Hope you are having a good time. Love Grandpa.'

"I've got to go out and buy a postcard," said Lionel.

"But you're going home next Thursday!" said Mrs Carrington.

"It isn't for Mum and Dad. It's for Grandpa. I promised, but I forgot. I've got to send it off today. And I'd better buy one for Linnet."

Mrs Carrington nodded. "Yes, I expect she's missing you. I was very impressed by the way she took care of you when you came here nearly two years ago. She's very fond of you."

"Sometimes you wouldn't think so," said Lionel. "You should hear her go on about some of the things I want to do."

"Well, I daresay that's just because she does care so much about you. Big sisters are all the same. And I can tell you're very fond of her."

"She's not bad," admitted Lionel, "she's got no confidence in me, that's all."

Mrs Carrington told him how to get to the shop, which was just a short way along the lane, and he set off. He hoped that Uncle Richard would be safe whilst he was away. Although most of his theories had collapsed he was still convinced that Mr Vowels, Mr Knight and Miss Baker were after something that Uncle Richard had got, which perhaps he was unaware that he had got – because he had said last night that he didn't know what they meant by the gold – and that they wouldn't give in until they had it in their own possession.

He found the shop without any difficulty, bought his postcards and stamps, and sat down on a bench outside the shop to write his messages on the back. To Linnet he wrote wittily, 'Having a good time, hope the mummies don't bite you, Love, Lionel.' And (having decided to send a card to Mum and Dad as well) he wrote, 'Went to the theatre last night and solved the mystery before Uncle Richard, Love, Lionel.' To Grandpa he wrote, 'Thanks for your card. I like the bridge. I've found out about Uncle Richard. Love, Lionel.' When he had posted the cards he started to walk back to Blooms Nurseries. He had covered half the distance along the lane when, turning a corner, he found himself overtaking Miss Baker! She was striding along very purposefully, in one hand a long walking umbrella which she used as a stick.

Lionel's heart began to thump. He kept behind her, glad of the fact that several people passed by, some on foot, some in cars or on bicycles. It was perfectly obvious that she was on her way to Blooms. Lionel had just made up his mind to run on ahead and warn Uncle Richard of her approach when she happened to glance round. It wasn't difficult to imagine that she must have heard his heart beating.

"Ah!" she said in her boisterous manner. "You're the boy I saw at the hotel yesterday." Lionel couldn't think how she had recognised him, because he had been disguised so well, but there was no denying it. "Picked up my scarf, I hear. Gave it to Vowels. Pity about that, but I suppose he would have seen me sooner or later. Never could tuck myself away in a corner and be unnoticed." And she gave a loud laugh.

Lionel couldn't think of anything to say, so he just walked along beside her hoping for an opportunity of slipping away from her when they came near the gate. He looked apprehensively at the umbrella. It looked like a perfectly ordinary umbrella, but he had heard stories of them being tipped with poison or even being guns in disguise.

Miss Baker went on, "I had no idea that Vowels was coming down to Dearmouth – nor Knight, for that matter. You should have seen Knight's face when he saw me – oh that was worth coming for if nothing else! Anyhow, Vowels returned the scarf, as you see, so I must thank you. I take it that you *are* the boy he mentioned – the one he said had picked up the scarf?"

Lionel nodded.

"Live around here, do you?"

"No. I'm on holiday."

"Anywhere near Blooms Nurseries?"

"Yes."

"In that case, perhaps you can help me. Do you know of a man called Richard Flaxby?"

"He's gone to Australia."

"What!" She stopped for a moment and stared into his face as if she would have pierced through to his brain.

"To farm sheep."

"When did he go?"

"I'm not sure."

She continued her walk. "You must be mistaken. His name's on the electoral roll. I checked yesterday. Blooms Nurseries. No question about it."

They had reached the gate by now and Lionel could see Uncle Richard in the distance making his customary morning inspection of the outdoor plants. Miss Baker saw him too, and pointed in triumph with her umbrella. Until that moment Lionel had forgotten that Uncle Richard had said he had met someone of the name of Baker.

"Flaxby!" she shouted, and when Miss Baker shouted there was no doubt of anyone with normal hearing being aware of it. "Flaxby, tracked you down again! I want a word with you!"

Desperately Lionel thought of some means of stopping her. He could go in with a Biffy Jardine tackle (Biffy Jardine's tackles were one of the reasons why Lionel hated school football so much, for he was a notoriously foul player), but he doubted if it would have much effect on Miss Baker's hefty legs; besides, he had a feeling that she would kick him right back, and that was no mean consideration. The best thing to do was run to Uncle Richard and tell him to flee for his life.

Before he had run ten paces, however, he realised that Uncle Richard had had the same idea, for he was making speedily for the little gate at the perimeter of the grounds, which Lionel knew gave access to the cliff path. For one brief moment Lionel had a pang of disappointment in his uncle for not turning and facing the danger like a man, but then he turned his head and saw Miss Baker right behind him and felt that few men would have cared to confront her in her present mood.

And he wasn't even a man yet! He was just a boy, and Miss Baker could flatten him with one hand. It was with tremendous relief that he suddenly saw Mrs Carrington emerge from behind a hedge with a bunch of onions in her hand.

"Yes?" she said to Miss Baker.

"I wanted to speak to Flaxby."

"He isn't here."

"I know that now. I saw him go. Stupid man! Well, you can tell him that I shall be back. Baker's the name, and I don't give up that easily. Tell him." And she strode off.

"What a rude woman!" exclaimed Mrs Carrington.

"Have you ever seen her before?" asked Lionel, aware that his legs were trembling.

"No, and I hope I shall never see her again," said Mrs Carrington, bending down to pick some radishes.

Lionel went back to the house. He felt disconsolate. Uncle Richard had run away and might not be back all day. He might never come back again now but find another hiding place, leaving his gardens to grow wild, his orchids to rot, and his greenhouses to decay. No, thought

Lionel, that wouldn't happen. He, Lionel, would see to that. He'd tell Mum and Dad and Grandpa and Linnet all about it, and they would come and see that everything was attended to – or would they? Wouldn't they say he was fantasising again? Couldn't he just hear Linnet's scorn when he told her that Uncle Richard was being hounded by a desperate gang? Would she *ever* accept that he was going to be a private investigator?

Only if he solved this mystery. Only if Uncle Richard was true to his word and would back him up. He squared his shoulders and went upstairs to his room. He took out his big notebook and headed a fresh page: NEPS GNAG. He laboured at his code for about half an hour, writing down everything that had happened since he had come to Dearmouth.

The telephone shrilling in the hall disturbed his thoughts. He waited for Mrs Carrington to answer it. The bell went on and on. She must still be out of the house. He ran downstairs and picked up the receiver.

"Hullo?"

"Hullo, Lionel?"

"Uncle Richard – where are you?"

"At The Silver Cliffs Hotel. Can you come and meet me?"

Lionel's heart leapt for joy. It was just like in the books! A secret meeting! "Yes," he said breathlessly.

"Take the cliff path. You don't want to bump into that odious woman again, do you?"

"No."

"Right. Meet me in the coffee lounge."

"Who was that?" asked Mrs Carrington, coming through the hall.

"Uncle Richard. He wants me to meet him."

"Oh, that's nice." She seemed to have no suspicion at all that things were becoming desperate. "Don't forget to tell him about that woman. Perhaps there was something wrong with some plants she bought. There was no need for her to be so ill-mannered, though." She went off into the kitchen and a moment later Lionel heard her singing to herself.

Lionel had walked the cliff path with Linnet when they had been there before, and he

remembered the way perfectly. It was a favourite walk of the tourists, winding down between
trees that were almost tropical to a pleasant park.
The Silver Cliffs Hotel must be somewhere near
the park. He hesitated before starting out. Did
he need a disguise of some sort? He settled for
a sweater he hadn't worn yet and brushed his
hair down over his forehead. One day he'd
experiment with hair dyes. And when he was
older he could have no end of fun with false
whiskers and toupees. He slipped out of the
house by the back door, skirted the entire
grounds, and went through the gate.

He soon reached the start of the cliff path,
which at first was bare and unshaded by trees
of any sort, but as it dropped into the lee of the
cliff the vegetation increased dramatically and
soon he was hurrying through a glade. All the
time he kept looking back to see if he was being
followed. And this proved to be very unwise.
He was so concerned about the possibility that
Miss Baker had spotted him going out of the
gate and might be following at a distance that
he didn't think that he might meet with a

member of the gang coming in the opposite direction. He almost bumped right into Mr Vowels.

"Well, Lionel," he said, as Lionel stood before him panting a little, "it seems that somebody has been leading me up the garden path."

Pretending not to understand what he meant Lionel said, "This is the cliff path."

"I'm aware of that. I also understand that there is a back approach to Blooms Nurseries along here."

Lionel could only nod his agreement.

"So I should like to have a little talk with that uncle of yours."

"He's not there," said Lionel defiantly as he spotted a family party approaching.

"Now don't tell me he's gone to Australia," Mr Vowels grinned, "because I know now that he hasn't. He's a cool customer, I must say, telling me that his name was Bloom."

"He didn't tell you that," said Lionel.

"No, you're quite right, he did not. It was the waiter chap who said that, but I was fool enough to believe the story about Australia." He broke into a laugh. "Sheep-farming! Well, young man, if he isn't at home, where is he?"

Lionel thought swiftly. He didn't want Mr Vowels turning back with him, for he would then, no doubt, go right back to the hotel, and that would lead him straight to Uncle Richard. "I mean he's not at the house," Lionel said desperately. "He's working in one of the greenhouses."

"Well, thanks," said Mr Vowels. "I daresay I shall see you again sometime, Lionel." He hurried off just ahead of the group of people who were toiling upwards and Lionel ran thankfully in the opposite direction. His troubles were not quite over yet, all the same, for he was taking the final flight of steps two at a time when he caught sight of Mr Knight slipping stealthily behind a tree.

"Seen my friend Mr Vowels?" he asked as Lionel came abreast of him.

"Yes," said Lionel, caring little now for Mr Vowels' warning not to disclose anything, "he's up there on the cliff path."

"Thanks," said Mr Knight.

What a day this was proving to be. He hadn't had so much action since his holiday in Spain, when he had been certain that somebody had put a bugging device in Dad's car. (Well, the foreign van *had* tailed them for miles and miles, hadn't it? And the sinister little man *had* ended up in the same hotel . . .)

He brought his mind back to the case in hand and looked around for the correct path to the hotel. He saw that the entrance was through the tennis courts. He was breathing quickly now because he had run practically all the way, but he knew that Uncle Richard must be waiting for him anxiously, so he ran on. He was pretty certain that the members of the gang were safely out of the way – unless Miss Baker had had a car tucked away somewhere and had attempted to cut Uncle Richard off somewhere. By the time he entered the hotel lobby he was sweating, very red in the face, and panting like a dog in hot weather.

The official whom he had seen there yesterday came up, but stopped a few feet away from him when he saw who he was. "You'll pardon me for saying so, young man, but I do think it's irresponsible of your parents or whoever is looking after you to let you come out in that state of health. Your temperature must be very high, very high indeed. You're dreadfully flushed, and mumps is so highly contagious . . ."

"I haven't got mumps," Lionel said. "It turned out to be something different, not catching at all." He peeled off his sweater and pointed to his neck. "See – no lumps? Can I see Mr Bloom?"

"Mr Bloom? Not Mr Vowels?"

"No, I have to see Mr Bloom."

"He's through there." The man indicated with his head a door with a frosted glass panel, and after giving Lionel a very strange look, disappeared through an archway.

Lionel pushed open the door of the coffee lounge. His face was set and serious. Uncle Richard must be desperately anxious to see him, possibly had something important for him to do. He was sure that when he saw his uncle he would find him pale, tense, almost despairing, completely dependent upon any help that he could give him.

But he was totally wrong. Uncle Richard was sitting at a table by the window, a coffeepot, cups and cream cakes in front of him, and when he saw Lionel his face creased into the biggest grin that Lionel had ever seen upon it. "Come and have some coffee," he said, "and as many cream cakes as you can eat. What do you make of it all now?"

Lionel sat down beside him. "Well, for one thing," he said, "I know why Mum used to call you Rocky."

Chapter Eight

THEY were walking along the beach. Uncle Richard had listened carefully to Lionel's frank confessions as to the possibility of his being a one-time crook, of his having something belonging to the people who were following him, and of his idea that he had a new valuable plant in his orchid house. He hadn't laughed or been offended at any of them.

"So you've disposed of all those theories," he

said, "and have arrived at the conclusion that the mystery revolves around my name."

"Yes," said Lionel.

"You're quite right, it does."

Lionel looked up at him with shining eyes. "I knew I was right!" he said. "Your real name is Rockingstone, isn't it?"

"Well, in a way it is. Think again, Lionel. Think hard. You saw my name in the book I left in your room, didn't you?"

"Yes."

"And what else have you seen about the place? I left another clue for you."

"You haven't made all this mystery up, have you? No, you couldn't have. You wouldn't set all those people to follow me and pretend to be desperate criminals." Lionel was thinking aloud. "I know – the other book – the scrap book all about Grandfather Flaxby. That's it, isn't it? The other clue's in there. Wait a minute," he said, as Uncle Richard started to interrupt him, "there was a date in there."

"You're doing fine."

"The date was your birthday. May 10th. That

was when the team won the cup."

"May 10th – what year?"

"Nineteen forty-eight, I think. Yes, I'm sure it was."

"A very auspicious day, wouldn't you say?"

Lionel stopped. Uncle Richard picked up a pebble and flung it into the ocean. He was smiling.

"Was that the day – the actual day when you were born?" asked Lionel.

"It was."

"You were born on the day that they won the cup? Grandfather Flaxby must have been over the moon!"

Uncle Richard nodded emphatically. "Practically unbalanced," he said. "Let's sit down."

They sat on the sand, Uncle Richard picking up pebbles and dropping them into his palm, Lionel squatting before him knowing that something very significant was soon to come. Uncle Richard threw a pebble as far as it would go. "Richard," he said. He threw another pebble. "Oliver," he said. Another. "Charles."

Lionel knew that his mouth had dropped

open but somehow he couldn't snap it shut again as Uncle Richard continued: "Keith Ian Norman George Sternway Timothy Overton Neil Edward – Flaxby."

"You mean –" Lionel gasped, "you mean Rockingstone isn't your name but your initials? You've got all those names?"

"That's right."

"Grandfather Flaxby named you after all the team members?"

"And even the trainer, to whom I am indebted for the Sternway. My father was totally obsessed with the game of soccer. He was a very good man," Uncle Richard hastened to say, "and an excellent father. I missed him very much when he died. But somehow I never inherited his love of sport, and I was always particularly uninterested by the game which provided me with my names. Can you imagine the ribbing I got when other boys discovered the truth behind Rockingstone? I was hounded by people who wrote newspaper articles with human interest, as they call it. I was asked to appear on television. I hated it all. For years I couldn't forgive my father, but as I got older I did understand how his enthusiasm must have carried him away. Those boys in the team were all orphans in whom my father had taken a strong interest – he was head of a special school – and their achievement must have elated him very much. I don't mind now. One doesn't mind these things as one gets older."

Lionel dug his hands into the sand. "And those people – Mr Vowels and the others – want to get you on TV? No, that's not it. Don't tell me. S.P.E.N. It's not nurserymen, it's something to do with names!"

"The Society of People with Extraordinary Names."

"They want you to join."

"They want me to become a brother of the society, to attend their secret meetings wearing purple robes, to swop stories about how they came to get their names, indulge in a lot of silliness that I'm simply not interested in. Miss Baker has been hounding me for years, and I think you can imagine that her image doesn't reflect very well on the society. Having seen something of the other two this week I'm inclined to think they're all a little bit mad."

"I was getting close, though, wasn't I?" Lionel said. "I'd have solved it before long."

Uncle Richard laughed and stood up. "Yes," he said, "you have tenacity and guts, I'll grant you that. Did you really believe they were out to kill me?"

"Well – yes, I was worried."

"Let's go and see if lunch is ready."

The full humour of the situation seemed to strike them when they came within sight of Blooms. They glanced at each other and began to laugh. They roared. They had to wipe the tears away. They were still laughing when they went into the house.

"Well," said Mrs Carrington, "I'm glad you two have found something to amuse you. I've been badgered to death all morning by people demanding to see you, and who wouldn't take no for an answer either. Such manners! That woman! I told them in the end that you'd gone over to Paddon Caves, and the only way they can get there is on foot over the sands, about three miles. *That* should keep them busy," she concluded with a grim smile.

Lionel was thoughtful over the meal. It was barely over when the phone rang. "It's your sister," said Mrs Carrington, holding out the receiver.

Lionel took it. "Hullo," he said, "found any daddies yet?"

"Hah-hah!" she responded. "How are you getting on?"

"Fine."

"Chest-high in some sort of mystery, no doubt?"

"Oh no," he said airily, "I solved that ages ago."

"Did you indeed? I'll bet you are giving Uncle Richard a bad time."

"Uncle Richard's fine. We're having great fun. I had a postcard from Grandpa this morning."

"Yes, so did I. Poor Grandpa. Aunt Essie seems to be getting worse. He telephoned me yesterday and she was waiting to clean the fingerprints off the phone after he'd finished with it. And she was in a bad mood because people keep coming to the front door instead of going to the shop. He says he won't stay much longer. I'm looking forward to seeing him again, aren't you?"

"Yes."

Uncle Richard came up. "Is that Linnet? Can I speak to her?"

Lionel said, "Uncle Richard wants to speak to you."

Uncle Richard said a few things that made her giggle, and then she asked if Lionel was causing any trouble. Lionel could hear quite clearly.

"Trouble?" said Uncle Richard. "I don't know what you mean."

"With his latest craze – this detective nonsense."

"I don't think it's nonsense at all," said Uncle Richard, winking at Lionel. "I think he's very good at it."

"What?"

"I think he'd make a jolly good private investigator."

Lionel grabbed the phone. "See?" he yelled.

"I see. Two of a kind as Mum says." But she parted from him with affection. Lionel turned to his uncle.

"Thanks," he said.

"Don't mention it."

"Does Linnet know your real name?"

"Good heavens, I hope not. Linnet couldn't keep a secret like that."

Lionel felt proud to have been entrusted with it. "I want to go out this afternoon," he said.

"Where would you like to go? We could go to Southampton, see the ocean-going liners."

"I want to go out alone. I have something to do."

Uncle Richard nodded. "Be back in time for tea," he said. He didn't ask any questions. He understood. He always did.

The tea dance was in progress when Lionel arrived at the hotel. He dodged the official man and slipped into the conservatory. Mr Vowels was sitting at a table by himself. Mr Knight was sitting at another. Miss Baker was prowling about the terrace keeping her eyes on both of them. They all perked up when they saw Lionel.

He went to Mr Vowels' table and sat down. "Uncle Richard isn't going to join you," he said bluntly. "You might as well give up."

Mr Vowels sighed. "I was afraid of that," he said. "Such a wonderful name. And so near the gold, too." He seemed ready to burst into tears and Lionel wondered how he could ever have believed him to be a desperate criminal.

"Mr Vowels," he said, "what is the gold?"

"The gold? Oh, the gold medal. We get a gold medal when we've recruited fifteen new members. And the right to wear a gold tie instead of this awful thing. We get to sit at the top table at the annual dinner. And – oh, so much more! Gold medallists are elevated so much higher than ordinary members." He sighed again. "I was so sure that I was going to get my gold before either Knight or Baker."

"Maybe you can," said Lionel, leaning close.

"What do you mean?" Mr Vowels' eyes flickered over to Knight and Baker.

Lionel went closer and whispered in his ear. A huge smile spread itself over the man's face. And he, too, whispered. Lionel chuckled. He shook Mr Vowels' outstretched hand. He chuckled all the way over to the french windows and almost exploded with laughter as he passed Miss Baker. Then he went and sat on the balustrade overlooking the grand entrance to the hotel.

After about half an hour, during which time the grin never left his face, Lionel saw Mr Vowels come out, followed by a porter carrying his bags. He got into a cab and was borne away. As the hotel porter went back towards the revolving doors Mr Knight came rushing out carrying his bag. He spoke urgently to the porter and placed something in his hand. The porter spoke to him and Mr Knight got into a cab and he, too, was driven off.

Lionel waited until he had seen the same procedure repeated by Miss Baker, then he jumped off the balustrade, put his notebook away – he had had important notes to make – and went whistling back to Blooms Nurseries.

"You look like a cat that's been at the cream," said Mrs Carrington as she poured tea.

"I have," said Lionel. He looked at Uncle

Richard, who was eyeing him quizzically. "You want to know what Mr Vowels' full name is?" he asked, pulling out his notebook.

"Yes," smiled Uncle Richard.

"Who is Mr Vowels?" put in Mrs Carrington.

"He's Anthony Everard Ireson Oswald Ulverton Vowels,' said Lionel.

Uncle Richard choked over his tea.

"Get it?" said Lionel.

Uncle Richard roared with laughter. "I get it," he said, and went on, "*I* should worry!"

Lionel had to explain it to Mrs Carrington.

"Well I never!" she said. She didn't seem to think it was funny at all.

"I know what Miss Baker's name is," said Uncle Richard, "if that's what you were going to tell me next. She told me when she came after me seven years ago. It's Queen Boadicea Baker."

Mrs Carrington sniffed. "Just what she deserves," she said.

"How about the other one?" asked Uncle Richard. "Mr Knight?"

Lionel said, "I'm not sure that I believe this

one. I think Mr Vowels might have been kidding me." He looked down at his notebook.

"Don't keep us in suspense," pleaded Uncle Richard.

"He said it was Wilden Stormie."

Uncle Richard grinned. "He must have been kidding," he said.

"More tea?" enquired Mrs Carrington.

"Yes, please."

"I'll have to go and fill up the pot."

When she had gone out of the room Uncle Richard said, "What have you been up to?"

"Just getting rid of them," said Lionel.

"How?"

"I sent them up to Newcastle." He paused. "To see Aunt Essie."

"Why?"

"Because she deserves them," said Lionel, thinking of Grandpa, "and her name is Sarah Selina Susan Serafina Shipstocks. That's why she's called Essie. Didn't you *know*?"

MIRACLE AT CLEMENT'S POND
Patricia Pendergraft

When Lyon and his friends find a baby abandoned by Clement's Pond it seems common sense to leave it on the doorstep of the poor old village spinster, Adeline, who has longed for a baby all her life. All the children think it's the perfect answer to the problem at the time, but as Lyon is to find out, there are unforeseen complications to follow.

LAURIE LOVED ME BEST
Robin Klein

Julia hates the hippie-like commune where her mother has taken them both to live. And Andre feels stifled by her father's rigid ways. Together they seek refuge in an abandoned cottage behind their school and begin to make it their ideal home. However, their private lives amazingly remain a mystery to each other, so when a gorgeous 18-year-old boy turns up, they're soon unwittingly competing for his charms.

ALLY, ALLY, ASTER
Ann Halam

Richard and Laura aren't very keen on making friends with the next-door neighbour's pale, cold daughter, Ally, when they move to the isolated cottages on Cauldhouse Moor. There's something strange, almost inhuman, about her. But it's only as the bitter winter winds and snow draw in around the bleak moors that Richard and Laura discover that Ally is more than a little icy . . .

SUMMER FOR A LIFETIME
Brigid Chard

Dan feels a failure, and when he is sent to his uncle's farm to recover from an operation, his confidence is at its lowest ebb. But soon not getting into his brothers' school ceases to seem so important as Dan's priorities change and his life finds a new direction. Who could have guessed at the thrill of snaring a rabbit, seeing a calf born, or training your very own ferret? Under the expert guidance of wily old ex-gamekeeper Ben Hugget, Dan develops skills he never dreamt he had and gradually learns a new self-respect.

THE MINERVA PROGRAM
Claire Mackay

Here at last is Minerva's chance to be out in front, to be really good at something – computers. That's where her future lies. But that future is threatened when Minerva is almost too clever for her own good. Suddenly she is accused of cheating and is banned from the computer room. It takes the combined talents of 'Spiderman', her brother, and her inventive friends to solve this intriguing mystery.

DREAM HOUSE
Jan Mark

For Hannah, West Stenning Manor is a place of day-dreams, but for Dina its attraction lies in the celebrities who tutor the courses there. But when a well-known actor arrives, hotly pursued by his attention-seeking daughter, Julia, Dina begins to realize that famous people are no better than ordinary ones. A warm and tremendously funny story by the author of *Thunder and Lightnings*.

THE SILK AND THE SKIN
Rodie Sudbery

What are Ralph and his gang always doing in the churchyard? Guy just *has* to find out, although it's obvious they're up to no good. He soon discovers that he and his backward younger brother are being drawn into a nightmarish situation. But where is Guy going to find the courage to stand up against Ralph and his gang and the forces of the supernatural they've already summoned . . .?

FINN MAC COOL AND THE SMALL MEN OF DEEDS
Pat O'Shea

Finn Mac Cool is the bravest, wisest, tallest and rudest of the warriors of the Fianna. Unfortunately, when the giant arrives to ask for his help Finn just happens to have a very bad headache. He is the only hope for saving the heir to the throne in the country of the giants so Gariv, the sly old servant, has to use all his wiles to get Finn on his feet and ready for battle.

RACE AGAINST TIME
Rosemary Hayes

From the moment Livvy sees the island, she knows there is something wrong. A strange and menacing force beckons, drawing her and her brother into a race against time. They are destined to fulfil an ancient quest to restore a magical cross to its rightful owner, but they must face the forces of unparalleled evil to do so.

ROSCOE'S LEAP
Gillian Cross

To Hannah, living in a weird and fantastical old house means having to endlessly fix things like heating systems and furnaces, but for Stephen it is a place where something once happened to him, something dark and terrifying which he doesn't want to remember but cannot quite forget. Then a stranger intrudes upon the family and asks questions about the past that force Hannah to turn her attention from mechanical things to human feelings, and drive Stephen to meet the terror that is locked away inside him, waiting . . .

OVER THE MOON AND FAR AWAY
Margaret Nash

The new girl at school calls herself a 'traveller' and says she comes from beyond the stars. Ben doesn't believe her, of course, but then again Zillah isn't quite like anyone he and his friends have ever met. There's her name for a start, and she doesn't even know how to play their games. But the mysterious newcomer does seem to be able to make things happen . . .

THE TROUBLE WITH JACOB
Eloise McGraw

Right from the start there is something very weird about the boy Andy sees on the hillside. Every time Andy's twin sister Kat is there he just disappears, and all he ever talks about is his bed! Andy thinks he's going mad, but then he and Kat decide that someone is playing tricks on them. There must be some logical solution to the mystery. After all, the only other explanation would be far too incredible . . .